Dear Parents:

Congratulations! Your child is taking the first steps on an exciting journey. The destination? Independent reading!

STEP INTO READING® will help your child get there. The program offers five steps to reading success. Each step includes fun stories and colorful art or photographs. In addition to original fiction and books with favorite characters, there are Step into Reading Non-Fiction Readers, Phonics Readers and Boxed Sets, Sticker Readers, and Comic Readers—a complete literacy program with something to interest every child.

Learning to Read, Step by Step!

Ready to Read Preschool–Kindergarten
• big type and easy words • rhyme and rhythm • picture clues
For children who know the alphabet and are eager to begin reading.

Reading with Help Preschool–Grade 1
• basic vocabulary • short sentences • simple stories
For children who recognize familiar words and sound out new words with help.

Reading on Your Own Grades 1–3
• engaging characters • easy-to-follow plots • popular topics
For children who are ready to read on their own.

Reading Paragraphs Grades 2–3
• challenging vocabulary • short paragraphs • exciting stories
For newly independent readers who read simple sentences with confidence.

Ready for Chapters Grades 2–4
• chapters • longer paragraphs • full-color art
For children who want to take the plunge into chapter books but still like colorful pictures.

STEP INTO READING® is designed to give every child a successful reading experience. The grade levels are only guides; children will progress through the steps at their own speed, developing confidence in their reading.

Remember, a lifetime love of reading starts with a single step!

Thomas the Tank Engine & Friends™

CREATED BY BRITT ALLCROFT

Based on The Railway Series by The Reverend W Awdry.
© 2015 Gullane (Thomas) LLC.
Thomas the Tank Engine & Friends and Thomas & Friends are trademarks of
Gullane (Thomas) Limited.
HIT and the HIT Entertainment logo are trademarks of HIT Entertainment Limited.
All rights reserved. Published in the United States by Random House Children's Books, a division
of Random House LLC, 1745 Broadway, New York, NY 10019, and in Canada by Random House
of Canada Limited, Toronto, Penguin Random House Companies.

Step into Reading, Random House, and the Random House colophon are registered trademarks of
Random House LLC.

Visit us on the Web!
StepIntoReading.com
randomhousekids.com
www.thomasandfriends.com

Educators and librarians, for a variety of teaching tools, visit us at RHTeachersLibrarians.com

ISBN 978-0-553-50747-8 (trade) — ISBN 978-0-375-97378-9 (lib. bdg.) —
ISBN 978-0-553-50748-5 (ebook)

Printed in the United States of America
10 9 8 7 6 5 4 3 2 1

HIT entertainment

THOMAS & FRIENDS™

AS SEEN ON DVD!
DINOS & DISCOVERIES

THOMAS AND THE VOLCANO

Based on The Railway Series
by The Reverend W Awdry

Illustrated by Richard Courtney

Random House 🏠 New York

It was a busy day
on Sodor.
The Earl was building
a Dinosaur Park!

The park had models

of dinosaurs.

They were not real.

But they looked real!

Each engine had a job.
Thomas and Millie
carried trees and bushes
to plant.

Samson and Harvey
helped put the dinosaur
models together.

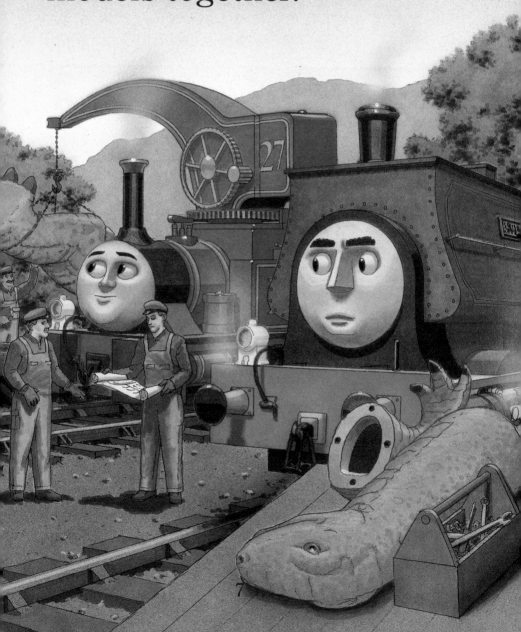

Suddenly, a dinosaur
head swung right
at Millie!

She screamed
and closed her eyes.
It stopped just in time!

Harvey and Samson
laughed at Millie.
"What a silly little
engine!" said Samson.

Millie was angry.
She tooted her whistle
and puffed away.

Millie wanted
to teach the big engines
a lesson.

But she and Thomas
had work to do!
They had to haul
wood for a bonfire.

Samson and Harvey
were working nearby.
They were building
a volcano.

13

"What is a volcano?"
asked Harvey.

"It is like a big firebox
filled with smoke
and lava!" Samson said.
Harvey was scared.

Millie heard
Harvey and Samson.
She had an idea.

"Build the bonfire
behind the volcano!"
she said to the workers.
Smoke rose into the sky.

Samson saw the smoke.

"The volcano is erupting!"

he cried.

Samson and Harvey
were scared!
They called for help
and sped away.
Millie's plan had worked!

Then the engines
heard Millie laugh.
"Silly big engines,"
she teased.
"It was just a trick!"

The Earl wanted
the tricks to stop.
The engines smiled
and agreed.

The engines kept
their promises.
They worked together.
They did not play
any more silly tricks.

The Earl was proud.
Soon the park was
ready for visitors.

What a team!